PUPPIES and PIGGIES

CYNTHIA RYLANT

Illustrated by IVAN BATES

Harcourt, Inc. · Orlando Austin New York San Diego London

www.HarcourtBooks.com

Library of Congress Cataloging-in-Publication Data
Rylant, Cynthia.
Puppies and piggies/Cynthia Rylant; illustrated by Ivan Bates.
p. cm.
Summary: Rhyming text describes what various animals do and what they love,
as well as a baby who loves his bed and his mother.
[1. Animals—Fiction.   2. Mother and child—Fiction.   3. Stories in rhyme.]
I. Bates, Ivan, ill.   II. Title.
PZ8.3.R96Pu 2008
[E]—dc22   2004003136
ISBN 978-0-15-202321-8

First edition
A C E G H F D B

Manufactured in China

The illustrations in this book were done on
Saunders Waterford paper with wax crayons and watercolors.
The display type was set in Eastman.
The text type was set in Cantoria.
Color separations by Bright Arts Ltd., Hong Kong
Manufactured by South China Printing Company, Ltd., China
Production supervision by Christine Witnik
Designed by Lydia D'moch

For Owen
—C. R.

For Grace
—I. B.

Puppy loves the farmyard,
Puppy loves the rain.

Puppy loves to press his nose
Against the windowpane.

Kitty loves a garden,
Kitty loves a rose.

Kitty loves to walk up high
On her kitty toes.

Bunny loves some lettuce,
Bunny loves some peas.

Bunny loves to hide herself
Among the apple trees.

Piggy loves his mud pen,
Piggy loves his slop.

Piggy loves the barn where he
Can roll around and flop.

Chicky loves her nesting,
Chicky loves her seeds.

Chicky loves to peck all day.
That's all Chicky needs.

Mousey loves to wiggle,
Mousey loves to hide.

Mousey loves a nice dark hole
To put himself inside.

Goosey loves his honking,
Goosey loves his walk.

Goosey loves to find a friend
And talk and talk and talk.

Pony loves a pasture,
Pony loves to run.

Pony loves to stretch her legs
In the summer sun.

Baby loves his blanket,
Baby loves his bed.

Baby loves his mama, who will
Kiss his sleepy head.

Happy piggies, happy puppies,
Happy babies, too.
Happy little lovey-doveys . . .

Just
like
YOU!